To my family. And to the memory of my aunt Mary, whose spirit
still lives and grows in her rosebush and in all of us. ~D. W.

For sweet Kalin, who loves roses ~L. P.

Text copyright © 2010 by Douglas Wood. Illustrations copyright © 2010 by LeUyen Pham. All rights reserved.

No part of this book may be reproduced, transmitted, or stored in an information retrieval system in any form or by any means, graphic,
electronic, or mechanical, including photocopying, taping, and recording, without prior written permission from the publisher.
First edition 2010. Library of Congress Cataloging-in-Publication Data is available.
Library of Congress Catalog Card Number 2008031687. ISBN 978-0-7636-1090-6 Printed in Shenzhen, Guangdong, China
This book was typeset in Kennerley. The illustrations were done in watercolor.
Candlewick Press, 99 Dover Street, Somerville, Massachusetts 02144. Visit us at www.candlewick.com
09 10 11 12 13 14 CCP 10 9 8 7 6 5 4 3 2 1

Aunt Mary's Rose

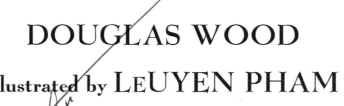

DOUGLAS WOOD

illustrated by LeUYEN PHAM

CANDLEWICK PRESS

I looked all over the rosebush in Aunt Mary's backyard, the bush she had asked me to water.

I looked at the blossoms. I looked at each petal. I looked at the leaves. At the stems. I even looked around the roots.

"Take care of this rose, Douglas," Aunt Mary had said, "and one day there will be a little bit of you inside of it. And a little bit of the rose inside of you."

I had just poured two pails of water on the rosebush, pulled out some crabgrass, and plucked off a couple of old blossoms and some yellow leaves.

Now I looked it over very carefully, and all I saw was . . . rosebush.

I ran inside to ask Aunt Mary, the screen door slamming behind me. Aunt Mary was at the kitchen counter, peeling apples, maybe for a pie, maybe for applesauce. Either one was fine with me.

"Aunt Mary," I said, catching my breath, "I looked and looked at that rosebush, and I'm not in it anywhere! I've been taking care of it for a week, and it's really pretty and there's two new blossoms, but I can't see me in it at all."

"Well, Douglas," she said, smiling, "it's not really something that you see. It's more something that you *feel,* sort of like—"

"Okay!" I shouted, and ran back outside to check, the screen door slamming again.

I dashed over to the rosebush once more. This time I felt a red blossom, soft and velvety. I felt some smooth green leaves. I felt the stem. Then I felt a thorn. In fact, I felt it a little bit harder than I meant to. That didn't help at all!

I ran back to the house, opened the screen door, and . . . Aunt Mary caught it before it slammed shut.

"I felt every part of that rosebush, Aunt Mary," I said, "and I'm not in it. I'm sure I'm not. And I don't think it's in me, either. I'd be able to tell. Look!" And I held up my finger, a tiny drop of blood on the tip.

Aunt Mary took my finger and held it under the cold-water faucet. Then she dried it, put a Band-Aid on it, and gave it a kiss.

"I've been taking good care of the rosebush, Aunt Mary. Really I have," I said. "But I don't think it's working at all. I don't think . . ."

Aunt Mary was chuckling. "Why don't you sit down, Douglas," she said, "and try to hold still for five minutes. I want to tell you a story."

Aunt Mary began. "You're not the only one who's in that rosebush, you know," she said.

"When I was a little girl growing up on the farm, my daddy asked me to take care of that rose. He said that he had helped to plant it years before, with his father. 'It's had a bit of a hard life, Mary,' he said, 'and it needs someone to look after it.' Then he told me that if you take care of something, a little bit of you begins to grow inside of it, and a little bit of it grows inside of you. 'Just like the sun and wind and rain help this bush to grow, so do you,' he said. 'Your hard work and your help, your weeding and watering and your gentleness and even your smile—all these things go right into it and help it grow. So in a way, you are in this rosebush. And as it grows and blossoms, some of that beauty grows inside of you.'

"And so, Douglas, I took care of the rosebush."

"Then one day, when I was nearly grown," Aunt Mary told me, "two little boys arrived at the farm. It was your dad, Jim, and his brother, Dick, my nephews. Something had happened, and they needed a place to live. 'You'll always have a place here,' my mother and father told them. And so they stayed with us."

"My daddy says that you were almost like their mother," I said. "That you woke him and Dick up in the mornings and got them ready for school, that you took care of them when they were sick and gave them haircuts right on this stool! He says you made them eat their vegetables and wash behind their ears and say their prayers, and that you read them stories and tucked them in at night. . . ."

Aunt Mary smiled. "Well, I guess that's right, Douglas. But that's what families do. They take care of each other. They love each other."

"Your daddy and Dick loved the farm," Aunt Mary continued. "They followed Grandpa out to the barn in the early mornings at milking time and helped him squirt milk into the cats' open mouths.

"Grandpa also showed them how to use a paintbrush and a hammer and how to whittle a stick into a whistle.

"With Grandma they helped to churn butter and hung it from a rope in the cistern.

"And they tagged along with me to pick plums and berries to make—"

"I pick berries with you too, Aunt Mary," I interrupted, "for pies or jelly!"

"That's right. You do," said Aunt Mary. "just like your daddy did."

And she patted my cheek.

"There came a day," said Aunt Mary, "when Grandpa couldn't milk the cows in the morning or take the boys for a ride in the car. And not very long after that, Grandpa wasn't with us anymore.

"I was out by the rosebush that day, when the boys came to find me. That's when I told them, 'You know, boys, there's a little bit of your grandpa in this rosebush, and there always will be.' And I explained to them what my father had told me. I told them that if they helped to care for it, they would be in it too, just like their grandpa, and it would grow inside of them."

"And did they help take care of it, Aunt Mary?" I asked.

"Yes, Douglas, they always did, from then on."

I smiled at Aunt Mary. I liked the idea of my daddy taking care of the same rosebush that I was taking care of now and of his grandpa still being somewhere inside of it.

"What happened then, Aunt Mary?" I asked.

"Well, Douglas, the years went by, and your daddy grew up, and so did Dick," she said.

"Did they have any adventures?" I asked. "Did they ever get into trouble?"

Aunt Mary laughed. "Well, there was the time when Dick started the windmill up while the workman was up there trying to fix it. And the time he put the cat down the outhouse hole, just to see what would happen. But he didn't mean any harm. And then there was the day your daddy slid down the barn roof just for fun and got a whole backside full of slivers, right through his britches. I had to pluck them all out, one by one, with Jim hollering 'ouch' so loud that Dick couldn't stand it and had to run outside.

"Mostly, though, they just liked to spend time together, to go fishing, and to play in the woods."

"But then there came the Depression, a time when nobody had much money. We couldn't afford to live on the farm anymore—Grandma and the boys and I—so we moved to a house in town. But before we left, we dug up the old rosebush and brought it with us. When we got to town, we planted it in the yard."

"Then what, Aunt Mary? What happened next?"

"Well, I worked in the general store and the post office, and I taught school. Of course, the boys went to school. I guess all the things that normally happen with boys happened. Sometimes they got sick, and Grandma and I took care of them. They went sledding and skating in the winter and played ball in the summer.

"Dick learned to play the trumpet, and your daddy played the guitar. As they got bigger, they worked on nearby farms for extra money. Mostly, they just spent lots of time together. They were best friends."

"And they took care of the rosebush, right, Aunt Mary?" I asked.

"That's right, Douglas. We all took care of the rosebush."

"Then one day your daddy wasn't a little boy anymore. He was a young man, and he went off to work his way through college to study music. Not long after, Dick followed him.

"But then came a terrible time. A great war began in faraway parts of the world. We hoped and hoped it wouldn't reach us, but finally it did. Your daddy signed up to serve, and later, so did Dick.

They went halfway round the world to do their part. Their grandma and I tried not to worry, but one day we got a letter telling us that Dick would not be coming back. Your daddy got the same letter where he was, too.

"And you know, Douglas, he told me that when he went to bed that night, he could almost feel his little brother beside him, just the way they had fallen asleep together so many times as children."

"Well, Douglas, your daddy made it home safely. He became a fine man, met your mother, and started his own family. And we're still taking care of that rosebush, aren't we? Because you see, our family is in it, and it's in us. And when I smell a blossom, or clip one and put it in a vase in the house, I feel close to all the people I love, and they're all still here. Do you understand?"

I nodded and said that I did. But I wasn't really sure.

Later that day, we sat at the kitchen table and had apple pie, with a rose blossom I'd clipped in the vase beside us. And the rose smelled so sweet, it almost seemed as if it was a part of the pie. And every good thing seemed a part of everything else.

"I love you, Aunt Mary" I said. Aunt Mary smiled.

"I love you, too, Douglas," she said. "And I always will."